For Ôliu — M.T.V.
For Wren — A.A.

Special thanks to Nipam Patel for sharing his expertise on butterflies.

To learn more about butterflies, check out some of the resources the author used while researching this book:

Burris, J., & Richards, W. (2006). *The Life Cycles of Butterflies: From Egg to Maturity, a Visual Guide to 23 Common Garden Butterflies* (2007 or Later Printing). Storey Publishing, LLC.
Discover Butterflies & Moths. (n.d.). Florida Museum. https://www.floridamuseum.ufl.edu/discover-butterflies/
How to attract butterflies to your garden. (n.d.). Natural History Museum. https://www.nhm.ac.uk/discover/how-to-attract-butterflies.html
Quirós, G. (2017, July 11). *Why Is the Very Hungry Caterpillar So Dang Hungry?* KQED. https://www.kqed.org/science/1811984/why-is-the-very-hungry-caterpillar-so-dang-hungry

Text © 2023 Mượn Thị Văn
Illustrations © 2023 Andrea Armstrong

Published in Canada and the U.S. by Kids Can Press Ltd.
25 Dockside Drive, Toronto, ON M5A 0B5

Kids Can Press is a Corus Entertainment Inc. company

www.kidscanpress.com

The illustrations in this book were created digitally.
The text is set in Ammy's Handwriting.

Edited by Yasemin Uçar and Sarah Howden
Designed by Andrew Dupuis

Printed and bound in Shenzhen, China, in 3/2023 by C & C Offset

CM 23 0 9 8 7 6 5 4 3 2 1

FSC
www.fsc.org
MIX
Paper | Supporting responsible forestry
FSC® C008047

LIBRARY AND ARCHIVES CANADA CATALOGUING IN PUBLICATION
Title: If you want to be a butterfly / by Mượn Thị Văn ; illustrated by Andrea Armstrong.
Names: Van, Muon, author. | Armstrong, Andrea, illustrator.
Identifiers: Canadiana (print) 20220453381 | Canadiana (ebook) 20220458383 | ISBN 9781525305467 (hardcover) | ISBN 9781525310287 (EPUB)
Classification: LCC PZ7.1.V36 Ifwa 2023 | DDC j813/.6 — dc23

Kids Can Press gratefully acknowledges that the land on which our office is located is the traditional territory of many nations, including the Mississaugas of the Credit, the Anishnabeg, the Chippewa, the Haudenosaunee and the Wendat peoples, and is now home to many diverse First Nations, Inuit and Métis peoples.

We thank the Government of Ontario, through Ontario Creates; the Ontario Arts Council; the Canada Council for the Arts; and the Government of Canada for supporting our publishing activity.

If You Want to Be a Butterfly...

Written by **Mượn Thị Văn**
Illustrated by **Andrea Armstrong**

Kids Can Press

If you want to be a butterfly,
then arise,
unfurl
and welcome
the waiting world ...

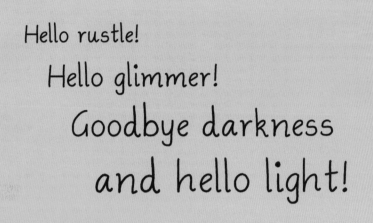

Hello rustle!
Hello glimmer!
Goodbye darkness
and hello light!

Hello warmth!
Hello rocks!

Goodbye roost
and hello tasty delights!
Hello dandelion,
hello sage!

Hello fennel,
hello milkweed!

Goodbye feast
and hello breeze!

Hello trees!
Hello hills!
Goodbye earth
and hello sky!

Hello sun!
 Hello!
  Hello!
   Hello everyone!

But before you can be a butterfly,
you must be a chrysalis.

If you want to be a chrysalis,
then hold on tight
and do not let go.

Do not let go
even if a fierce wind blows.

Do not let go
even if birds peck your shell.

Do not let go
even if you don't feel so well
and your insides begin to swell.

Do not let go
until a tiny voice comes along
like the first few notes
of a brand-new song:

HEY, IT'S FINALLY TIME.
HAS THE WORLD BEEN WAITING LONG?

But before you can be a chrysalis,
you must be a caterpillar.

If you want to be a caterpillar,
then never say *Please*
and never say *Thank you*
and always demand *More! More! More!*

Never use a fork
and never use a spoon,

and always lick
the itty-bitty leaf crumbs
from your itty-bitty thumbs.

Never eat less
than what you weigh,
and always weigh more
than the day before.

But most of all,

never,

ever,

EVER

share —

unless, of course,
there's something tastier
ELSEWHERE.

But before you can be a caterpillar,
you must be an egg.

If you want to be an egg,
then be very, very still.
And very, very small.

Close your eyes
and dream.

Dream of the smooth leaf
you have yet
to nibble.

Dream of the sweet flower
you have yet
to smell.

Dream of the blue sky
you have yet
to see.

Even big dreams
start out little
at first.

But before you can be an egg,
you must first be a ...

From Tiny Egg to Soaring Butterfly

A butterfly is beautiful to behold, but its transformation from tiny dreamer to soaring highflier might be even more magnificent.

A butterfly's life cycle begins as a little *egg*. The egg, laid by an adult female butterfly, is usually attached to a leaf. This egg is pretty tiny — sometimes no bigger than the head of a pin.

egg

When the egg hatches, an even tinier *caterpillar* crawls out. Right away, the caterpillar knows what it needs to do: eat, eat, eat! It often starts by eating the eggshell and then moves on to the leaves or other parts of the plant it hatched on.

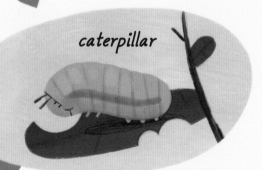

caterpillar

butterfly

After a couple weeks (though sometimes it can be months or even years in harsh climates), the chrysalis splits open and a full-grown **butterfly** emerges! First, the butterfly pumps its wings up and down to dry and expand them. Then it is able to fly, find food and reproduce. Some butterflies migrate long distances for food and warmer weather. Monarch butterflies travel as far as 5000 km (3000 m), while painted lady butterflies may travel 6500 km (4000 m) or more!

chrysalis

When the caterpillar grows too large for its skin, it sheds it — this is called *molting*. The caterpillar keeps eating, growing and molting until it has molted several times. Then it forms a hard, protective shell around itself, called a **chrysalis**. Inside the chrysalis, the caterpillar goes through a lot of changes. Its stomach shrinks, its wings appear and new parts, such as its straw-like mouth, form.

Butterflies are found on every continent except Antarctica, and they play an important part in ecosystems. During all stages of their lives, they serve as a food source for many types of animals. As adults, they pollinate our plants so that new plants can grow. Because they are highly sensitive to weather and climate, butterflies help scientists understand climate change and other shifts in the environment.

We can help butterflies by conserving their natural habitats and keeping wild areas wild. We can also plant nectar flowers that attract butterflies in our gardens and grow the plants butterflies lay eggs on and caterpillars munch.